Printed in United States
First Edition
10 9 8 7 6 5 4
ISBN 0-7868-3810-8
Library of Congress Catalog Card Number: 2005921137

For more Disney Press fun, visit www.disneybooks.com

Walt Disney's Cinderella

Disney Press

New York

Once upon a time in a faraway land, there lived a widowed gentleman and his little daughter, Cinderella. A kind and devoted father, he gave his beloved child every luxury and comfort. Still, he felt she needed a mother's care, and so he married again, this time to a woman with two daughters just Cinderella's age: Anastasia and Drizella.

It was upon the good man's untimely death, however, that the Stepmother's true, cruel nature was revealed. She was bitterly jealous of Cinderella's charms, and so were her daughters.

As time went by, their stately old chateau fell into disrepair. The family fortune was squandered upon the vain and selfish stepsisters, while Cinderella was forced to become a servant in her own home.

Yet through it all, Cinderella remained ever gentle and kind. And with each new dawn, she found hope that someday her dreams of happiness would come true. . . .

One particularly brilliant morning, Cinderella was awakened from her happy dreams, as she was most every morning, by the twittering of bluebirds.

"Cinderella," they sang in her ear. "It's time to wake up!"

Cinderella yawned and stretched and reluctantly sat up. "I know it's a lovely morning," she said with a sigh. "But it was a lovely dream, too."

As she began to unbraid her hair, she thought about how dreams were sometimes all that kept her from sinking into despair. Ever since her father's death, she had been treated like a slave by her stepmother and nasty stepsisters. To forget her troubles, she often dreamed of falling in love and leaving her horrible home behind. And because dreams were all she had, she never stopped believing in them.

Cinderella smiled at the birds and mice who had gathered in her room. They were the only real friends she had. Then the loud ringing of the bells in the palace clock tower sounded, and Cinderella rolled her eyes.

"I hear you!" she groaned, walking over to the window and glaring at the clock. "'Come on, get up!' you say. Even the clock orders me around. Well, there's one thing no one can order me to do. They can't order me to stop dreaming. And perhaps one day," Cinderella added wistfully, "my dreams really will come true."

With the help of her animal friends, Cinderella quickly straightened her attic room and put on an old brown dress. Then she tied back her golden hair, put on her apron, and prepared to face another day of cleaning and obeying the endless demands of her ungrateful stepfamily.

She was about to leave her room when two mice darted in, waving their arms and squeaking frantically.

"Wait a minute. One at a time, please," Cinderella said. She turned to one of the pair, a skinny mouse dressed in red. "Now, Jaq, what's all the fuss about?"

"There's a new mouse in the house," Jaq said. "A visitor."

Cinderella smiled. "How nice." She opened the drawer where she kept little clothes that she sewed for the mice. "He'll need a jacket . . . and shoes. . . ."

"He's in the trap!" Jaq announced urgently.

"The trap!" cried Cinderella. She rushed out of the room with the mice at her heels, straight to the mousetrap at the bottom of the stairs.

"Poor little thing," said Cinderella, opening the door. "He's scared to death."

"Don't worry," Jaq reassured the trembling mouse as he led him out of the trap. "Cinderella is our friend."

Cinderella smiled and offered the newcomer the tiny outfit she had chosen. "We have to give you a name," she said warmly. "How about Octavius? Gus for short!"

The mouse smiled back at her and nodded.

Then it was time for Cinderella to get to work. She hurried to the kitchen, leaving Jaq in charge of warning Gus about the dangers of his new home: namely, the Stepmother's mean old cat, Lucifer!

Lucifer, in fact, was the first of Cinderella's unpleasant daily chores. Every morning, Cinderella would quietly crack open the door to her stepmother's bedroom and call out softly, "Here, kitty, kitty."

Usually, the fat black cat would yawn and sneer, then turn around and settle back down on his bed again.

"Lucifer, come here!" Cinderella would hiss impatiently. Only then would the cat get up and slowly make his way across the floor.

"I'm sorry if Your Highness objects to an early breakfast," said Cinderella. "It's certainly not my idea to feed you first. I'm just following orders. Now, come on. To the kitchen."

There, Cinderella prepared the morning meal for all the creatures of the household—from the faithful old dog Bruno, to the chickens in the yard.

"Breakfast time!" she'd call. "Everybody up!"

This meant breakfast for Jaq and Gus and the other house mice, too. They scurried around the yard, gathering up as much corn as they could carry to their holes. Gus, in fact, was so intent on collecting his breakfast, he didn't even notice the dark shadow looming over him. Not until Lucifer pounced did Gus realize the cat was there. Instantly, the mouse dropped his load of corn and darted into the kitchen, racing up onto the table and ducking behind an empty cup.

But Lucifer was right behind him. He grabbed the fragile teacup and slammed it down on top of the mouse. Then Lucifer's mouth stretched into an evil grin. He had Gus right where he wanted him.

Claws at the ready, the cat had just begun to lift the cup when a shrill bell rang out. "Cinderella!" an even shriller voice called out. "Where's my breakfast?"

Startled, Lucifer dropped the cup just as Cinderella scooped up the three tea trays she had prepared, including the one on which Gus was trapped.

"Coming!" she called, hurrying out of the kitchen. All Lucifer could do was follow close behind.

Cinderella climbed to the second floor and entered the first door in the hall. "Good morning, Drizella," she greeted her stepsister. "Sleep well?"

"Hmmph!" Drizella grumbled. "As if you cared." She snatched one of the trays from Cinderella's hands, then dumped a basket of wrinkled clothing at her feet. "Take that ironing and have it back in an hour," she ordered.

"Yes, Drizella," said Cinderella. Balancing the basket on one hip, she left the room and moved down the hall to the next bedroom.

"Good morning, Anastasia," Cinderella said as she stepped into the room.

"Well, it's about time," Anastasia muttered. She shoved a box into Cinderella's arms. "Don't forget the mending. And don't be all day getting it done, either!"

"Yes, Anastasia," Cinderella said.

She hurried down the hall to the third room and opened the door. Inside, the chamber was dim and forbidding.

"Don't just stand there," her stepmother's voice called out from the darkness. "Put that down. Then pick up the laundry and get on with your duties."

"Yes, Stepmother," Cinderella answered. Arms full of ironing and mending and laundry, she backed out of the room and shut the door behind her. Cinderella was almost to the stairs when a terrible scream rang out.

Lucifer turned and raced to Anastasia's closed door, grinning in anticipation. As the girl continued to shriek, Gus ran out from under the door—and into the cat's waiting paws.

"Mother!" Anastasia howled, running into the old woman's bedroom.

Then Drizella emerged from her room, shooting Cinderella a withering glare. "*Now* what did you do?" she snapped.

Cinderella could hear Anastasia shouting, even through the Stepmother's closed door. "She put it there! A big, fat, ugly mouse! Under my teacup!"

Cinderella turned to stare suspiciously at Lucifer. "All right," she said. "What did you do with Gus?"

Slyly, Lucifer opened his empty paws and smiled. Then Cinderella lifted him up by the scruff of his neck . . . and there, quivering under his hind foot, was Gus.

"Poor thing," said Cinderella as the mouse scooted into the nearest hole. "Lucifer," she sighed, "won't you ever—"

But before she could finish, her stepmother's bedroom door opened, and the cat fled inside. The stepsisters came out, sneering.

"Hmmph!" Drizella grumbled.

"Are you going to get it!" said Anastasia nastily.

"Cinderella," her stepmother called out. "Come in and close the door."

"Surely, you don't think that I—" Cinderella began.

"Hold your tongue," ordered her stepmother. "It seems we have time on our hands," she said. "Time for vicious practical jokes. Perhaps we can put that time to better use."

Cinderella wasn't sure what was coming next, but she knew she wouldn't like it.

"Now, let me see," her stepmother said. "There's the large carpet in the main hall—clean it! And the windows, upstairs and down—wash them!"

"But I just finished—" Cinderella pleaded.

"Do them again!" her stepmother interrupted. "And don't forget to weed the garden, scrub the terrace, sweep the halls and the stairs, and clean the chimney. And of course, there's still the mending, ironing, and laundry to be done." She paused for a breath and took a sip of tea. "Oh, yes, and one more thing . . . see that Lucifer gets his bath."

As Lucifer frowned in annoyance, Cinderella sadly walked out of her stepmother's room. Despite all her wishes and dreams, why did it seem as if her life kept getting worse?

Meanwhile, inside the palace, the portly, white-haired king was slumped on his royal throne.

"It's high time my son got married and settled down," he proclaimed to his closest adviser, the Grand Duke.

"Of course, Your Majesty," the Grand Duke answered. "But we must be patient."

"I am patient!" the King shouted. "But I'm not getting any younger. I want to see my grandchildren before I go." He wiped a tear from his eye. "I want to hear the pitter-patter of little feet again."

"Now, now," the Grand Duke comforted him. "Perhaps if we just let the Prince alone . . ."

"Let him alone!" the King bellowed. "Him and his silly romantic ideas?"

"But, sire," the Grand Duke protested, "in matters of love—"

"Love!" The King cut him off. "Ha! What is love? Just a boy meeting a girl under the right conditions. So, we must simply arrange the conditions."

"But—but, Your Majesty," the Grand Duke stammered. "How?"

"Bah!" replied the King. "The boy is coming home today. What could be more natural than a ball to celebrate his return? And if all the eligible maidens in my kingdom just happened to be there, he'd be bound to show interest in one of them. Wouldn't he?" The King giggled happily, imagining the scene. "It can't possibly fail!"

"Very well, sire," the Grand Duke said. "I shall arrange the ball."

Later that morning, Cinderella was scrubbing the chateau's stone floor when an urgent knock called her to the door.

"Open in the name of the King," a voice boomed. Cinderella opened the door, and a messenger handed her a large white envelope. "An urgent message from His Majesty." Then the messenger spun on his heel and hurried away.

As Cinderella turned from the door, she gazed curiously at the letter. Just then, Jaq and Gus asked in unison, "What's it say?"

"I don't know," Cinderella replied. "But he said it's urgent. I'd better take it up right away."

Cinderella carried the letter to the music room, where her stepsisters were having their daily music lesson. She hesitated a moment, then stepped into the room.

"Cinderella! I've warned you never to interrupt us," her stepmother immediately scolded.

"But this just arrived—from the palace," Cinderella explained.

"From the palace!" Like flies to honey, the stepsisters lunged for the sealed letter.

"*I'll* take it," their mother said. She snatched the envelope and opened it, her eyes growing wider as she read. "Well," she said at last, "it seems there's to be a ball."

"A ball!" Anastasia and Drizella shrieked in unison.

Their mother nodded. "In honor of His Highness, the Prince. And by royal command, every eligible maiden is to attend."

"'Every eligible maiden' . . ." Cinderella said thoughtfully. ". . . Why, that means that I can go, too."

"Ha!" Drizella laughed. "*You? Dance with a prince?*"

"Well, why not?" Cinderella said. "After all, I am a member of the family. And it does say 'by royal command.'"

"Yes, so it does," said her stepmother slowly. "Well, I see no reason why you can't go—"

"Mother!" Drizella and Anastasia argued.

"—*if,*" their mother went on, "*if* you get all of your work done . . . and *if* you can find something suitable to wear."

"Oh, I'm sure I can!" cried Cinderella, hurrying joyfully out of the room. "Thank you!"

"Mother!" Drizella complained. "Do you realize what you just said?"

"Of course," her mother replied coolly. "I said '*if*'!"

Up in her room, Cinderella pulled a cloud of bright pink silk out of a trunk at the foot of her bed. As she held it up, the fabric unfurled into a long, fancy gown. Still holding the dress in front of her, she whirled around the room, imagining what it would be like to dance the night away at the ball.

"Isn't it lovely?" Cinderella said to the crowd of mice and birds who had gathered around her. "It was my mother's."

The animals looked on in awe. "Beautiful!" one of the mice exclaimed. "But it looks kind of old."

"Well, maybe it is a bit old-fashioned," Cinderella admitted. "But I can fix that."

She pulled a pattern book out of her sewing basket and thumbed through the pages. "There ought to be lots of good ideas in here."

"That's a nice one," said one of the mice as Cinderella pointed to a page.

Cinderella nodded thoughtfully. "Of course, I'll need a sash and a ruffle and—"

"Cinderella!" a voice suddenly cried.

She sighed and put down the pattern book. "Oh, now what do they want? I guess my dress will have to wait."

"Poor Cinderella!" cried Jaq as he watched her leave the room. "She won't be able to go to the ball. They'll make her work, work, work. Cinderella will never get her dress done in time!"

"Poor Cinderella," Gus agreed sadly.

Then a mouse named Blossom scampered over to the open book. "*We* can do it!" she piped up. "*We* can help Cinderella fix her dress!"

Eager to help Cinderella, Jaq and Gus ran off to collect some trimmings. Peeking into Anastasia's room, they could see Cinderella's stepfamily giving her yet more chores.

"Mend the buttonholes! Press my skirt! Mind the ruffles— you're always tearing them!"

Cinderella tried not to cry as garment after garment was heaped onto her arms. Then Cinderella's stepmother said, "And when you're through with all that, I have a few more little things for you to do."

Sadly, Cinderella mumbled, "Very well," and walked away.

But Anastasia and Drizella were not done complaining. "I don't see why everybody else has such nice things to wear and I always end up with these old rags," Anastasia whined. She tossed aside a pretty pink silk sash. "Why, I wouldn't be seen dead in this!"

"She should talk," Drizella said. "Look at these beads!" She threw a sparkling necklace on top of the sash. "Trash! I'm sick of them!" And with that, they marched out of the room.

As soon as the door closed behind them, Jaq and Gus hopped out from behind a chair and ran over to the unwanted trimmings.

"We can use these!" Jaq squeaked in delight.

They scooped up the treasures and hurried back to Cinderella's room, where the other mice and birds had already started working. Jaq and Gus proudly draped the pink silk sash around the dress, and two birds tied it into a big, fancy bow. Then more birds laid the gleaming strand of beads around the collar.

Slowly but surely, the dress took shape. Thanks to her friends, Cinderella would be able to go to the ball after all! And maybe, just maybe, her dreams would finally come true.

As evening fell, every maiden in the kingdom was atwitter with excitement. Every maiden, that is, but one.

Cinderella stood in the upstairs hall, gazing forlornly out the window. She had finished her chores. But there had been no time for her to fix her dress, and the carriage was due any moment to take the family to the ball.

Cinderella sighed. It just wasn't fair. She worked so hard and asked for so little. . . . But where was the sense in hoping for something that was never meant to be? Just then, the gleaming black carriage pulled up to the front of the chateau. Cinderella sighed once more, then went to fetch the others.

"The carriage is here," she announced as she entered the parlor.

"Why, Cinderella," said her stepmother, pretending to be surprised. "You aren't dressed for the ball."

"I'm not going," she said softly.

"Oh, what a shame!" cooed her stepmother, turning to smile triumphantly at her two smug daughters.

"Yes," said Cinderella, choking back tears. "Good night." And she raced up to her room. Once there, she gazed out the window at the dreamy palace glittering on the horizon.

"Oh well, what's a royal ball?" she said, trying to sound brave. "After all, I suppose it would be frightfully dull . . . and boring . . . and completely . . . *wonderful*."

Then suddenly the room lit up behind her, and Cinderella spun around to find the most beautiful dress she had ever seen.

"Surprise!" exclaimed the mice and birds.

"Oh, how can I ever thank you?" she cried.

Quickly, she changed into her new gown, then glanced out the window. The carriage was still there! "Wait!" she cried, hurrying down the stairs. "Please! Wait for me!"

Her stepmother and stepsisters were nearly out the door when Cinderella reached them. "Isn't it lovely?" she exclaimed, twirling in her new gown. "Do you think it will do?"

Anastasia and Drizella glared at Cinderella. "Mother!" both girls cried.

"Girls! Please!" the Stepmother shouted. "After all," she said more calmly, "we did make a bargain. And I never go back on my word." Then she cast a long, hard look at Cinderella. "How very clever, these beads," she said. "They give it just the right touch. Don't you think so, Drizella?"

"No," huffed Drizella. "I think—" Then suddenly she recognized the beads she'd thrown away. "Why you little thief!" she screeched. "They're my beads! Give them here!" And she reached out and ripped the beads off Cinderella's neck.

"And that's my sash!" shouted Anastasia.

"Please! Don't—" begged Cinderella as Anastasia tore at her skirt. But the two sisters kept pulling and clawing and tugging . . . until Cinderella's once lovely dress was nothing but shreds.

Blinded by tears, Cinderella dashed out of the house and deep into the garden. There, she threw herself onto a bench and buried her face in her arms.

"It's no use," she sobbed. "No use at all! There's nothing left to believe in . . . nothing!"

"Nothing, my dear?" a melodious voice asked. "Oh, now, you don't really mean that."

"Oh, but I do!" Cinderella insisted. She lifted her head and caught her breath. A moment ago the garden had been dark and deserted. But now, a smiling, white-haired woman with a halo of sparkling light was beside Cinderella.

"Nonsense, child," she said. "If you had lost all of your faith, I couldn't be here. But, as you can see, here I am! Now, dry those tears. You can't go to the ball looking like that."

"The ball?" Cinderella repeated, tears welling once more in her eyes. "I'm not going to the ball."

"Of course you are," the woman said. "But we'll have to hurry. Even miracles take a little time, you know."

"Miracles?" Cinderella asked in confusion.

"Just watch," the woman said. "Now . . . what in the world did I do with my magic wand?"

"Magic wand," Cinderella echoed in amazement. "Why, then, you must be—"

"Your fairy godmother, of course!" the woman said. And with a wave of her hand, she magically produced a wand from thin air. "Now, let's see. I'd say the first thing you need is"— her eyes scanned the garden— "a pumpkin!" She pointed to a big, round pumpkin at the edge of the garden and waved her wand: "Bibbidi-Bobbidi-Boo!"

Wide-eyed, Cinderella watched as the pumpkin shivered . . . and jumped . . . and was suddenly transformed into a gleaming silver coach.

"Now," the Fairy Godmother continued. "To draw an elegant coach like that, of course, we'll simply have to have . . . mice!"

And with another wave of her wand, she turned Gus and Jaq and two other mice into sleek, white horses. Then she turned the old family horse into a coachman, and the faithful old hound, Bruno, into a well-dressed footman.

At last, the Fairy Godmother turned to Cinderella. "Well, hop in, my dear. We musn't waste time."

Cinderella glanced down at her ragged dress. "Uh . . ."

"Now, don't try to thank me," the Fairy Godmother said.

"Oh, I wasn't," Cinderella began. "I mean, I do! But . . ."

Finally, the Fairy Godmother took a good look at Cinderella's tattered gown. "Good heavens, child!" she exclaimed. "You can't go in that!"

One last time, she waved her magic wand, sang out the magic words, and transformed Cinderella's rags into a shimmering ball gown.

When the magic dust settled, Cinderella looked exactly like a princess, from her beautiful upswept hair to the dainty glass slippers on her feet.

"Why, it's like a dream come true," she said in delight. "A wonderful dream come true!"

"Yes, my child," said the Fairy Godmother. "But like all dreams, I'm afraid this one can't last forever. You'll have only until midnight, and then the spell will be broken. Everything will be as it was before."

"I understand," said Cinderella. "But it's so much more than I ever hoped for."

"Bless you, my child," said the Fairy Godmother, and she waved Cinderella into the coach.

At the palace, the grand ballroom was already crowded with maidens from all over the land. As each young lady entered the hall, the royal chamberlain announced her and introduced her to the Prince, who tried his best to stifle his bored yawns.

"The mademoiselles Drizella and Anastasia," announced the chamberlain as Cinderella's stepsisters made their way to the front of the line.

The Prince bowed politely. But as he straightened up, his gaze wandered past them to another young lady who had just entered the hall.

He stared, transfixed. She was truly the most beautiful girl he had ever seen. Pushing past the startled stepsisters, he made his way toward the lovely new guest.

Cinderella was still in awe of the beauty and grandeur of the palace, but the sound of approaching footsteps soon brought her back to reality. She looked up and caught her breath as she gazed into the eyes of a tall young man. When he smiled kindly and asked her to dance, she was stunned—and delighted.

Of course, she'd been hoping to catch a glimpse of the Prince, but she quickly decided that that could wait. After all, how could the Prince be more handsome or charming than this young man?

She returned his smile and gave him her hand. As he swept her off in a waltz, she felt as if they had been dancing together all their lives, and she knew without his saying so that he felt just the same. They hadn't even exchanged names . . . and yet, they were falling in love. And the whole ballroom noticed!

"Who's that dancing with the Prince?" Anastasia pouted. "I feel as though I've seen her before."

With narrowed eyes, Cinderella's stepmother watched the couple dance. "There is something familiar about her," she said. But before she could get a closer look, the Prince swept Cinderella out the door.

Out in the royal gardens, Cinderella and the Prince danced across the terrace, then strolled hand in hand across a little bridge. They turned to each other, their eyes filled with love, and happily shared a long, tender kiss.

Then suddenly, the clamoring of chimes pierced the calm night. Cinderella glanced up at the clock tower. "Oh, my goodness!" she exclaimed. "It's midnight!" She remembered the Fairy Godmother's warning and pulled away from the Prince's embrace.

"Good-bye," she whispered as the clock struck again.

"No! Wait! You can't go now," the Prince protested.

"But I must," Cinderella replied.

"But why?" the Prince asked, confused.

Desperately, she searched her mind for an excuse. "Well, I, uh, I haven't met the Prince yet." Then she turned and hurried back toward the palace.

"The Prince?" he repeated. Could she really not have known that *he* was the Prince? "Wait! Come back!" he called. "I don't even know your name."

As the clock continued to strike, Cinderella raced through the ballroom past the Grand Duke, who quickly joined the Prince in his chase. But Cinderella was halfway down the steps and into her waiting coach by then. In her haste, a glass slipper had fallen off one of her dainty feet. But it was too late to fetch it. The clock was nearly done chiming—and she had to get away!

At the stroke of midnight, the Fairy Godmother's spell was broken. The coach turned back into a pumpkin, and all the animals turned back into their old selves as well. Hearing the palace guards approach, Cinderella and her animal friends hid in the brush at the side of the road.

As the guards' horses sped down the road, their thundering hooves smashed the pumpkin into pieces. But the guards didn't see Cinderella.

"I'm sorry," Cinderella told her friends. "I guess I forgot about the time. But it was so wonderful! And he was so handsome! And when we danced . . ."

She smiled at the memory. "I'm sure the Prince himself couldn't have been more charming."

That's when she spotted, peeking out from under her tattered dress, one sparkling glass slipper! Cinderella looked up at the starry sky, thinking of the kind fairy godmother. "Thank you!" she cried out joyously. "Thank you so very much . . . for everything!"

The next morning, the Grand Duke stood nervously outside the King's bedroom. Summoning all his courage, he knocked on the door. The King had left the ball soon after the Prince and Cinderella had started dancing, so he didn't yet know about the girl's hasty exit. More than anything, the Grand Duke wished he didn't have to be the one to break the news.

"Come in!" the King commanded.

Slowly, the Grand Duke opened the door. The King was stretching and wiping the sleep from his eyes. "So," he said to the Grand Duke, "has he proposed already? Tell me all about it. Who is she? Where does she live? Have you started arrangements for the wedding?"

"Er . . . I'm sorry, sire! I'm afraid she got away," the Grand Duke blurted out.

The King's face turned crimson. "She *what?*"

"I tried to stop her," the Grand Duke told him, "but she vanished into thin air." His hand trembled as he pulled Cinderella's shoe out of his pocket. "All we could find was this glass slipper. The Prince has sworn he'll marry none but the girl who fits it."

Furiously, the King snatched the slipper. Then his face began to soften. "Then," he began, "you will try this on every maiden in the land. And as soon as you find the one whom this shoe fits, we will have the biggest wedding this kingdom has ever seen!"

It didn't take long for the news to spread, and for Cinderella's stepmother to spring into action.

"Anastasia! Drizella! Get up, quick!" She charged into their rooms and roused them from their slumber.

"What's going on?" Anastasia asked groggily.

"The whole kingdom's talking about it," her mother told her. "Hurry now. He'll be here any minute."

"Who?" Drizella asked.

"The Grand Duke," her mother explained. "He's hunting for that girl, the one who lost her slipper at the ball. They say the Prince is madly in love with her—"

Crash! The Stepmother and her daughters turned to see Cinderella in the doorway, a tea tray overturned at her feet. The Prince! She had fallen in love with the Prince!

"You clumsy little fool!" cried her stepmother. "Clean that up! And help my daughters dress."

"If he's in love with that girl, what good does getting dressed up do us?" said Anastasia grumpily.

"Now, you two listen to me," said their mother. "There's still a chance that one of you can get him. No one knows who that girl is. The glass slipper is the only clue. And the Grand Duke has been ordered to try it on every girl in the land. If one can be found whom the slipper fits, then by the King's command that girl shall be the Prince's bride."

"His bride!" the sisters shrieked.

"His bride . . ." Cinderella softly echoed.

Then, Anastasia and Drizella began shouting order after order at Cinderella. But she just stood there staring into space. Surely, *this* was a dream, a wonderful dream.

"What's the matter with her?" Anastasia grumbled.

"Wake up," snapped Drizella. "We've got to get dressed."

Finally, Cinderella came out of her daze. With a burst of happiness, she realized she wasn't dreaming after all. The handsome, charming Prince really wanted to marry her!

"Dressed," said Cinderella happily. "Oh, yes, we must get dressed." And without another word, she danced out of the room, humming the tune of a waltz from the night before.

"Mother, did you see what she did?" Drizella whined.

"Are you just going to let her walk out?" Anastasia demanded.

"Quiet!" their mother snapped. She recognized the tune Cinderella had been humming. Could it be? she thought in horror. Could Cinderella be *the* girl?

Well, she thought to herself, that didn't mean she couldn't stop her. Silently, she followed Cinderella to her room, and with a twisted snarl on her jealous face, slammed the door behind poor Cinderella and turned the key.

"Please!" Cinderella begged, running and tugging in vain at the locked door. "You can't do this! You just can't."

Ah, thought her stepmother, but I can! And she did.

Cinderella's mouse friends looked on miserably as Cinderella threw herself down, sobbing, on her bed.

"We've got to get that key," Jaq said. "We've just got to!" So along with Gus, he slipped under the door and followed the Stepmother downstairs.

"Mother! He's here," Drizella shouted.

"Do I look all right?" asked Anastasia.

"Now, remember, girls," their mother warned. "This is your last chance. Don't fail me." Then she hurried to open the door.

A royal footman stood at the threshold. "Announcing His Imperial Highness, the Grand Duke!"

Cinderella's stepmother smiled and bowed. "May I present my daughters, Drizella and Anastasia."

The Grand Duke peered at the ugly stepsisters and shuddered. "Charmed, I'm sure," he said, though he was already quite certain that neither of them could be *the* girl.

Beside him, the footman presented the glass slipper.

"Why, that's my slipper!" shrieked Drizella.

"What?" cried Anastasia. "It's *my* slipper!"

"Girls! Girls!" their mother scolded. "Remember your manners. A thousand pardons, Your Grace," she said to the Grand Duke.

Meanwhile, Gus and Jaq had climbed up on the table closest to the Stepmother and were inching their way toward the pocket of her skirt. Inside, they knew, lay the key to Cinderella's room. Ever so carefully, Gus lowered Jaq into the pocket.

"Let us proceed with the fitting," declared the Grand Duke.

"Of course," the Stepmother agreed. "Anastasia, dear," she called, motioning her daughter to a chair.

Anastasia daintily pulled back the hem of her dress and grinned as the footman slid the slipper smoothly onto her foot.

"There!" she said triumphantly. "It's exactly my size."

But as she was talking, the footman lifted her foot higher to reveal that the slipper was really resting on just one of her toes.

"Oh, well," said Anastasia, her face turning bright red. "It may be a trifle snug today. You know how it is . . . dancing all night."

But no matter how hard she tried, she could not force her knobby foot into the tiny slipper. Her mother even bent over to help her push, and that's when Jaq—and the key—came tumbling out of her pocket. Luckily, Anastasia and her mother were so busy struggling with the shoe, they didn't even notice. Staggering under the weight of the big brass key, Jaq and Gus headed for the stairs.

The Grand Duke had just moved on to Drizella when Cinderella heard a sound outside her door. She peeked through the keyhole to see two little mice and one shiny key.

Cinderella's face lit up. But her smile quickly faded when she heard a crash and Lucifer's smug face came into view. He had Gus—and the key—trapped under a bowl.

"Lucifer! Let him go!" Cinderella pleaded. "Please!"

Hearing her cries, a whole army of Cinderella's animal friends came to the rescue. Mice hurled forks as if they were spears at the sly cat. Birds flew overhead, dropping dishes on his head. Still, despite their best efforts, Gus and the key remained trapped.

"Bruno! Get Bruno!" Cinderella called.

Two bluebirds flew off, and minutes later Bruno came charging up the stairs. That did it—Lucifer took one look and ran for his life. Then three of the strongest mice lifted up the bowl, freeing Gus, who dragged the key under Cinderella's door.

Back downstairs, Drizella was hollering at the footman, "I'll do it myself. I'll make it fit!"

And to everyone's surprise, after a good bit of moaning and squeezing, she did manage to cram her foot into the shoe. "There!" she exclaimed, holding it out for inspection.

"It fits?" the Grand Duke exclaimed. But suddenly Drizella's tortured toes uncoiled. The too-tight slipper shot off her foot and flew into the air.

The Grand Duke and the footman both lunged to catch it before it crashed to the floor—instead landing on the floor themselves. Horrified, the Grand Duke watched the slipper fall through the air . . . down . . . down . . . down. Desperately, he reached out his hand . . . and caught it on his finger.

"I'm dreadfully sorry, Your Grace," said the Stepmother. "It won't happen again."

"Precisely, madam," the Grand Duke replied. He stood up and brushed himself off. "These are the only young ladies of the household, I hope—er, I mean, presume."

"There's no one else," the Stepmother assured him.

As he turned to go, a gentle voice called out from the stairs. "Your Grace! Please wait!"

All eyes turned to Cinderella. "May I try it on?"

"Pay no attention to her," the Stepmother told the Grand Duke. "It's only Cinderella, our maid."

But the Grand Duke ignored her. "Come, my child," he said.

As soon as Cinderella was seated, the footman came running with the precious slipper. Suddenly, an evil smile crossed the Stepmother's face. She stuck out her cane . . . and tripped the footman!

With a heavy thud, the footman fell to the floor, and the slipper shattered into a million pieces.

"Oh, no, no, no!" groaned the Grand Duke. "This is terrible! What will the King say?"

"Perhaps," Cinderella spoke up softly, "if it would help—"

"No, no," the Grand Duke moaned. "Nothing can help now."

Cinderella only smiled. "But you see," she said, "I have the other slipper." She pulled the glass shoe's twin out of her pocket and handed it to the Grand Duke.

As her stepmother and stepsisters looked on in shock, the Grand Duke carefully slid the slipper onto Cinderella's foot. Naturally, it fit perfectly, and both he and Cinderella laughed with delight.

Cinderella didn't even notice her stepfamily's jealous scowls. The face of the charming Prince filled her mind instead, and her heart brimmed over with the knowledge that she would never be unhappy again.